little Miss Busy

by Roger Hargreaves

Little Miss Busy loved nothing more than to be hard at work, keeping herself busy.

As busy as a bee.

In fact, as busy as a hive of bees.

Every day she would get up at three o'clock in the morning.

Then, Little Miss Busy
would read a chapter from her favourite book.

It was called:
"Work is good for you".

And then she would get down to the housework.

She would begin by tidying up,
and then sweeping,
and dusting,
and scrubbing,
and polishing,
until everything was spotless.

She would clean her house from top to bottom
and then from bottom to top, just to make sure.

She even dusted the bread and polished the butter.

She wasn't happy unless she was busy working.

And she didn't rest all day long, not for a minute,
not even for a second.

From three o'clock in the morning
until after midnight.

That was until last Monday.

Little Miss Busy wasn't up at three o'clock.

She wasn't up by six o'clock.

She wasn't even out of bed by nine o'clock.

She was ill.

"Oh, calamity!" she cried.

"I won't be able to do any work!"

She telephoned Doctor Make-you-well.

Five minutes later he was at her bedside.

He asked her to put out her tongue.

He examined her throat.

And he looked at her hands and feet.

"What you need is rest, a lot of rest,"
he said, with a broad smile.

"A lot of rest," repeated Little Miss Busy to herself.

"Oh, calamity!"

There was a loud THUMP!

Which was the sound of Little Miss Busy
falling over backwards,
on to the bed,
luckily for her.

On Tuesday, Mr Strong
called to see Little Miss Busy.

He brought her 72 eggs.

Go on, count them.

"There is nothing like eggs
for giving you strength," said Mr Strong.

By the seventy-second egg,
Little Miss Busy was feeling much better.

That was, until Mr Strong said,
"Now you must rest to get your strength up."

There was a loud THUMP!

Which was the sound of Little Miss Busy
falling over backwards,
on to the bed,
luckily for her.

On Wednesday, Mr Greedy
came to visit.

He brought an enormous bowl of food.

"I always find that eating a big meal
makes me feel better," said Mr Greedy.

Little Miss Busy ate the lot.

She felt better than ever.

That was until Mr Greedy said,
"Now you must rest to let your stomach settle."

There was a loud THUMP!

And you know what that was, don't you?

That's right!

Little Miss Busy had fallen over backwards.

On Thursday, Mr Nonsense
popped in to see Little Miss Busy.

He brought her...an umbrella!

"Hello," he said.
"I hear you're feeling well. You don't need a rest..."

Little Miss Busy jumped for joy, right out of bed.
"...you need a holiday!" finished Mr Nonsense.

There was a loud THUMP!
That's right.
"There you look better already," said Mr Nonsense,
and left...

...by the open window.

Little Miss Busy picked herself up.

A small smile formed on her face.

Something Mr Nonsense had said
had actually made sense.

She had never thought of going on holiday before.

The more she thought about it the happier she felt.

She thought of all the fun things she could do.

There was the planning and organising,
there was all the shopping she would have to do,
there was the packing,
and she would have to learn the language,
and read lots of books about the place she was going to.

What a lot of work!

Little Miss Busy smiled happily.

The following Thursday, she was awake at three o'clock in the morning.

Everything was ready.

Little Miss Busy had had one of the busiest weeks of her life.

Which is saying something!

She had only one thing left to do.

And that was...

...to learn how to twiddle her thumbs!

Fantastic offers for Little Miss fans!

Collect all your Mr. Men or Little Miss books in these superb durable collectors' cases!
Only £5.99 inc. postage and packing, these wipe-clean, hard-wearing cases will give all your Mr. Men or Little Miss books a beautiful new home!

Keep track of your collection with this giant-sized double-sided Mr. Men and Little Miss Collectors' poster.
Collect 6 tokens and we will send you a brilliant giant-sized double-sided collectors' poster! Simply tape a £1 coin to cover postage and packaging in the space provided and fill out the form overleaf.

STICK £1 COIN HERE
(for poster only)

cut along the dotted line and return this whole page

Only need a few Little Miss or Mr. Men to complete your set? You can order any of the titles on the back of the books from our Mr. Men order line on 0870 787 1724. Orders should be delivered between 5 and 7 working days.

--- TO BE COMPLETED BY AN ADULT ---

To apply for any of these great offers, ask an adult to complete the details below and send this whole page with the appropriate payment and tokens, to: MR. MEN CLASSIC OFFER, PO BOX 715, HORSHAM RH12 5WG

☐ Please send me a giant-sized double-sided collectors' poster.
AND ☐ I enclose 6 tokens and have taped a £1 coin to the other side of this page.

☐ Please send me ☐ Mr. Men Library case(s) and/or ☐ Little Miss library case(s) at £5.99 each inc P&P

☐ I enclose a cheque/postal order payable to Egmont UK Limited for £........................

OR ☐ Please debit my MasterCard / Visa / Maestro / Delta account (delete as appropriate) for £........................

Card no. ☐☐☐☐ ☐☐☐☐ ☐☐☐☐ ☐☐☐☐ ☐☐☐☐ Security code ☐☐☐

Issue no. (if available) ☐ Start Date ☐☐/☐☐/☐☐ Expiry Date ☐☐/☐☐/☐☐

Fan's name: .... Date of birth: ....

Address: ....

....

Postcode: ....

Name of parent / guardian: ....

Email for parent / guardian: ....

Signature of parent / guardian: ....

Please allow 28 days for delivery. Offer is only available while stocks last. We reserve the right to change the terms of this offer at any time and we offer a 14 day money back guarantee. This does not affect your statutory rights. Offers apply to UK only.

☐ We may occasionally wish to send you information about other Egmont children's books. If you would rather we didn't, please tick this box.

Ref: LIM 001

cut along the dotted line and return this whole page